PUFFIN BOOKS

THE TALE OF PRISTINE CHRISTINE

"Annie Badger," wailed her Grannie. "How many times do I have to tell you NEVER . . . I repeat NEVER put your elbows on the table!!"

"Sorry, Grannie. Um . . . WHY NOT?" said Annie.

Grannie sat back in her chair and folded her hands on her lap – so began the tale of Christine Pristine, the neatest, cleanest, tidiest, pristinest girl in the whole world. She was voted Queen in her home town, Speen, and was invited for a crowning luncheon in the magnificent Speen Golden Parlour inside the Town Hall. Everything could have beenperfect, if only she had not put her elbows on the table!

A hilarious modern cautionary tale, and a perfect cure for all those of you who have the very bad habit of putting your elbows on the table.

Laura Beaumont lives in North London in a big orange house with a small blonde child and a little bearded man. She has been writing and illustrating children's books for two years and is very pleased to have finally discovered what it is she wants to be when she grows up.

Laura Beaumont

The Tale of Christine Pristine

or why you should never put your elbows on the table

Illustrated by Mary Rees

PUFFIN BOOKS

For Bill and Rosie

PUFFIN BOOKS

Published by the Penguin Group
Penguin Books Ltd, 27 Wrights Lane, London W8 5TZ, England
Penguin Books USA Inc., 375 Hudson Street, New York, New York 10014, USA
Penguin Books Australia Ltd, Ringwood, Victoria, Australia
Penguin Books Canada Ltd, 10 Alcorn Avenue, Toronto, Ontario, Canada M4V 3B2
Penguin Books (NZ) Ltd, 182–190 Wairau Road, Auckland 10, New Zealand

Penguin Books Ltd, Registered Offices: Harmondsworth, Middlesex, England

First published by Andersen Press 1991
Published in Puffin Books 1992
1 3 5 7 9 10 8 6 4 2

Text copyright © Laura Beaumont 1991
Illustrations copyright & Mary Rees 1991
All rights reserved

The moral right of the author has been asserted

Printed in England by Clays Ltd, St Ives plc
Set in Times

Annie Visits Her Grannie

Every fortnight, on a Saturday at 3.30 p.m.,
Annie went to her Grannie's house for tea.
Annie's Grannie was very old, very old-
fashioned and very particular indeed about
keeping things spick and span. She didn't
approve of all 'these new-fangled-dangled
technical gadgets' that everybody seemed to
be using these days . . . like televisions and
radios and tin openers.

If I want to watch the television I'll get an old shoebox and put the hamster in it with a bow tie on.

she used to say.

she used to say.

"Thanks Grannie . . ."

4

So, it goes without saying, that when Annie was at her Grannie's house she had to behave very primly and very properly indeed.

5

Now, this was very difficult for Annie because she wasn't by nature a very prim and proper girl – quite the opposite in fact. Annie was what some people might call a *tomboy*. This meant that she enjoyed doing *boyish* things more than she enjoyed doing *girlish* things.

Actually, if the truth were known, Annie enjoyed doing boyish things more than most of the boys she knew.

So you can imagine what a problem those fortnightly Saturday afternoons were.

Wash those tattoos off.

You are not taking that splurge gun.

9

Well, Saturday arrived just as it always did and Annie set off for Grannie's, taking care to disguise herself in case she was spotted by any of her friends wearing the stupid dress.

Grannie had laid the tea out on the table. It was the usual selection of brown lumps on plates. Oh yes . . . another thing

Grannie didn't approve of was food that tasted nice.

Her motto was:

"*If it tastes yummy keep it out of your tummy,*" which explained why everything she cooked tasted like scouring pads and coconut matting.

When Annie arrived, Grannie was in the middle of embroidering this motto onto a small square of cotton, which she would then frame and put on the wall. The writing was in the middle, and all around the outside were little clusters of root vegetables. Grannie embroidered a lot of root vegetables. She considered a pair of crossed turnips and a leek much more pleasing to the eye than a bunch of fussy old flowers.

The grandfather clock chimed at 3.30 p.m. and Annie and Grannie sat down to tea. They sat where they always sat, at either end of the small table.

Tea at Grannie's house was completely different from tea at Annie's. At home, Annie could lie on her back on the floor eating biscuits out of the packet if she wanted to. But at Grannie's there seemed to be as many rules and regulations for eating tea as there were for playing cribbage: sit with your back straight; eat with your mouth closed; never use the sugar spoon to stir your tea; always stick your little finger out when you hold a teacup; the list was endless and Annie tried very hard to remember everything, but it wasn't always that easy.

"So . . ." Grannie looked across at Annie and laid a serviette across her lap. She was about to ask whether Annie's parents had thrown the television onto the bonfire yet, when suddenly her expression changed. Her eyes flashed downwards, her mouth began to shake and her nose began to twitch. Her face looked like this:

except it was wobbling.
(*To get the full effect, waggle the book around*.)

Then she spoke.

"Elbows!" she hissed.

"I beg your pardon, Grannie?" said Annie, who thought she'd managed to remember everything she was supposed to do.

"ELBOWS! Get those elbows off my table this instant!" Annie looked at her elbows. They were indeed on the table. She quickly took them off. Grannie reached for the smelling salts.

"Annie Badger," she wailed. "How many times do I have to tell you NEVER . . . I repeat NEVER put your elbows on the table!!"

Annie looked down nervously.

"Er . . . sorry, Grannie, I forgot."

"Well, don't forget again!" Grannie put down the smelling salts, smoothed over her napkin, and was about to get back to the subject of the television and the bonfire, when Annie spoke again.

"Grannie?" she said.

"Yes Annie?" snapped Grannie.

"Um . . . WHY NOT?"

"WHAT!?" Grannie's face looked as if it was about to start wobbling again.

"Why not?" shrugged Annie. "Why shouldn't I put my elbows on the table?"

"WHY NOT?" said Grannie, flabbergasted that such a question should be asked. "WHY NOT? I'll tell you WHY NOT my inquisitive young madam . . . I'll tell you WHY NOT!"

Grannie took a deep breath. Annie leant forwards, her eyes widening in anticipation.

Grannie's eyes flickered momentarily as if she was trying to remember. Then suddenly she spoke again.

"Because of Christine Pristine, that's WHY NOT."

"Christine Pristine?" said Annie.

"Yes!" smiled Grannie triumphantly, "because of Christine Pristine."

Grannie sat back in her chair and folded her hands on her lap. And from the far away look in her eyes, Annie knew that a tale was about to be told . . .

Christine Pristine

"Christine Pristine," began Grannie, "was the neatest, tidiest, cleanest, pristinest girl that anyone had ever met. She had never once, in the whole of her life, made any kind of mess whatsoever.

When she did some painting she covered the entire house with plastic bin bags, just in case any of the paint splashed anywhere; when she finished playing with her dolls she took all their clothes down to the dry cleaners; and when she arrived home from school she looked neater and tidier than when she had left that morning.

She had never spilt or dropped or dripped or slopped *anything*, unlike all the other children at school, who wouldn't actually go home until they had managed to get a splodgy mark on every single article of clothing they were wearing . . . and anything that happened to be in their duffle bags.

So, it goes without saying that Christine Pristine didn't have very much in common with other children . . . especially at school playtimes. While they were all rolling about in the mud or seeing who could get the biggest grass stain, Christine would be standing alone in the smooth corner of the playground. The bit where nobody else played . . . because it wasn't dirty enough.

All the parents had heard of Christine Pristine and they begged their children to bring this marvellous, neat, tidy child home for tea . . . but nobody ever did. Nobody liked her. She was about as popular as the

man who stood on the corner of Pooley
Street shouting rude words and sticking his
tongue out at everyone.

But it wasn't just Christine's neatness and
tidiness that got on everyone's nerves. Oh
no, the reason why everyone disliked her so
much was that she always had this most

horrible, smug,
smirky expression
on her face . . .
like this:

. . . and the only thing she ever said to anyone was this:

'I'm neat and ti-dy and yo-or no-ot.'

Of course there were secrets to Christine's neatness and tidiness like:

(a) She never ate anything that was a different colour to whatever she was wearing, which, considering her school uniform was blue and grey, sometimes made things very difficult indeed.

(b) She would carry an iron and ironing board with her at all times in case her clothes got creased.

(c) She had a special device which she had invented herself called the 'choc'n'bogey detector'.

This was a ring with a tiny mirror on it that she could hold up to her nose and mouth and check for bogeys round the nose or chocolate round the mouth.

Christine also bathed three times a day, brushed her hair every five minutes and cleaned her teeth until she could see her face in them.

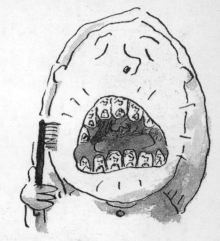

(This was another way of checking for bogeys and chocolate.)

Christine had actually inherited her neatness and tidiness from her mother, a fine woman, who, as the years went by, had got so worried about getting dirty that she now only went out when she was wearing a special protective suit that she'd designed herself.

Mrs Pristine called this protective suit *The Pristine Clothes Coverall* and she'd had lots of them made: ladies' ones, men's ones, smart ones for the evening and casual ones for a weekend in the country. They

were all made out of a glorious floral plastic
that you could wipe clean with a damp
cloth.

She then bought a little shop in the town
centre and tried to sell them.
Unfortunately, it seemed that not
everybody was as bothered about getting
dirty as Mrs Pristine . . .

. . . and in the four years that she had The Coverall Shop, she only ever sold two . . . and one of those was to her husband.

The Pristines lived in a little town called Speen and every year Speen crowned its own Queen. She was called the Speen Queen.

This was a very great honour and every year it was bestowed for a different reason. One year it would be for Speen's politest girl, then another year it might be for Speen's most nicely-spoken girl, but this particular year it was going to be given to

Speen's neatest
and tidiest girl.
So, guess who
won it? Well there
was no contest.

Well, I thought
I did rather
well....

The nearest
anyone else came
was little Lucy Shooker
who had managed to
keep her socks pulled
up for longer than three
hours.

So this year's title was to be Queen Clean
of Speen and the winner was Christine
Pristine.

Christine's mother and father were so
overjoyed when they heard the news that
they nearly split their coveralls . . . and do
you know what Christine said?"

Annie shook her head.

"She said: 'I'm neat and ti-dy and yo-or
no-ot.'"

Annie put her hand over her mouth
in horror.

Grannie continued, "there was a week to

go before the crowning and the 'phone
never stopped ringing. It seemed that as
soon as Christine was crowned, her life,
and indeed her parents' lives, would change
completely.

People wanted
her to do interviews
for newspapers . . .

. . . appear on
early morning
chat shows . . .

... and advertise their products ...

... and there were countless offers of round-the-world cruises, new cars, wardrobes full of clothes and all the soap she could use ... and believe me, Christine Pristine could use a lot of soap.

The day of the Speen Queen Crowning was always a very special day in the Speen calendar. There were lots of parades and

street parties and everyone in Speen looked
forward to it.

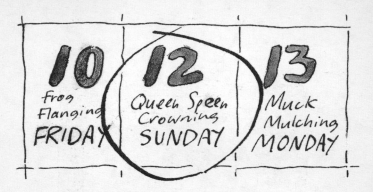

One of the most exciting things about
being crowned Queen of Speen was that
you got to see the famous Speen Golden
Parlour. The Speen Golden Parlour was
inside the Town Hall and was only ever
opened once a year for the Speen Queen
Crowning Luncheon. This was because it
was very special. In fact, it was considered
to be one of the three wonders of South
West England, along with the Hanging
Baskets of Biddle and the Mysterious
Oblongs of Ting.

It was called the Golden Parlour because
of its incredible gold painted wall carvings
and its spectacular ceiling. The ceiling was

painted like a huge sky, around which
floated clusters of golden clouds, hosts of
fat lady angels and a selection of grinning

chubby cupids, who wore nothing more than a few small floaty, wispy things that just about covered up their rude bits.

In the middle of the ceiling hung the huge Speen chandelier. There was gold leaf wallpaper on the walls and golden nails in the floorboards. But, most impressive of all was Speen's finest treasure . . . THE SPEEN SPLEEN . . . a solid gold replica of the spleen of the first ever wild boar to have been killed in Speen, and it must have been a biggun . . ."

"What's a spleen, Grannie?" interrupted Annie, looking quizzically across at her grandmother.

"It's an organ of the body situated to the left of the stomach, involved in maintaining the proper condition of the blood," said Grannie.

"Oh," said Annie.

Grannie sighed and continued, "as I was saying, the Spleen dangled from the ceiling of the Golden Parlour, held by a single golden cord.

The Speen Queen Crowning Luncheon
was a very important occasion and the
cream of Speen society had been invited.
Everyone had been instructed to wear their
finest finery, and if they didn't (and the
Town Hall had records of the contents of
all of their wardrobes, so they would know
if they weren't) they would be turned away
by the Wardrobe Wardens and never
invited again. THAT was how important an
occasion it was.

But the highlight of the day would almost
certainly be the crowning itself. Christine
was to be presented with a crown, a sash
and a long satin cloak by last year's Speen
Queen, a certain 'Queen Smart Porker',
who'd won her title for keeping Speen's
smartest pigs. (Christine had already
checked that the crown, sash and cloak
would be soaked in some very strong
disinfectant before she had to wear them.)

If the truth were known, Queen Smart
Porker wasn't altogether overjoyed at
having to hand over her crown, sash and
cloak, especially to someone as smug and

smirky as Christine Pristine and she'd been working very hard at making her pigs even smarter in the hope that she could keep the title for another year.

Once crowned, Christine would then sit on a shining golden throne in the middle of a flower-decked float. The float would then be pulled through the town by a large Speen shire horse, whilst primary school children danced around it dressed as root vegetables."

"Grannie . . ." warned Annie, who was well aware of her Grannie's affection for root vegetables.

"Alright . . . flowers!" snapped Grannie. "They were dressed as flowers.

The Big Day

Soon the big day arrived and Christine was so excited she had twenty baths, cleaned her teeth until she could see everyone's faces in them and put a new cover on her ironing board.

She had chosen to wear her best green satin dress which had been washed, pressed and starched a dozen times and then passed under a microscope for any sign of dirt or grime. Her mother and father got out their very best *Pristine Clothes Coveralls* and bought two new smart hats.

As the Pristines arrived at the Town Hall in a chauffeur-driven Rolls Royce, the Speen Bagpipers were standing in a line playing the Speen Queen Welcoming Song. The local townspeople stood around in clusters, waving flags and cheering, and teams of camera crews and photographers were getting set up, ready for the crowning.

Queen Smart Porker had brought along a selection of her smartest pigs (just so everyone could see how much smarter they'd become) and they were all standing in a gold-sprayed pigpen at the entrance to the Town Hall looking very smart indeed.

Everyone that had been invited had turned up and no-one had been turned away for not wearing their finest finery, although there was a rather embarrassing incident involving Lord Scrickett-Ground. As he'd arrived, the Wardrobe Wardens had quietly taken him to one side and suggested that, according to their records, the rather furry manky-looking thing he was wearing on his head wasn't actually the best hat in his wardrobe. It was then quickly pointed out by Lady Scrickett-Ground that the 'rather furry, manky-looking thing' was in fact a wig he wore to cover up his bald patch.

Without doubt, the most exciting guest of all, apart from the Mayor and Mayoress, of course, was a real-life television celebrity. This year they'd managed to get the man who presented a show called *Who's Trousers?*

In *Who's Trousers?* the presenter had to hold up a pair of trousers and a celebrity panel had to guess which famous person they belonged to.

If they didn't guess within sixty seconds they were allowed to go through the pockets.

Christine shook hands with the Mayor and Mayoress and told them that she was neat and tidy and they weren't. Then they all filed into the Golden Parlour. Everyone gasped in wonder at the very gold and rather green sight that met their eyes.

You see, Christine had requested that as she was wearing green, everything on the menu should be the same colour. So there was much muttering and jittering as the guests walked across to their seats past piles of green bread rolls, green butterpats, bowls of mint sauce, baskets of crisp green lettuce and tumblers full of gleaming lime cordial, all laid out around green crystal glasses, green Irish linen napkins and some very attractive green root vegetable arrangements . . ."

"Grannie . . ." warned Annie.

"No, these actually *were* root vegetable arrangements Miss Clever Clogs . . . the Mayoress was very partial to parsnips . . ."

"Sorry Grannie . . ."
muttered Annie.

"Anyway," continued
Grannie, "the centrepiece
of all this was the life-size
moulded greengage jelly of
this year's Queen of Speen,
Christine Pristine.

On the walls above
the table hung
portraits of all the
Speen Queens past
and present. Queen
Smart Porker sat
beneath hers, a rather
odd painting that
showed her standing
in a pig's trough with
a rasher of bacon in
one hand, a pork
sausage in the other
and a jar of apple
sauce on her head.

(The portraits by Mr Dally, the Speen Portrait Painter, had been getting stranger by the year. Quite a few people thought this might have something to do with a course of tablets he'd been taking for an elbow complaint.)

On one side of the Golden Parlour were two doors that flipped inwards and outwards. These flippy-floppy doors lead to the kitchen and sombre-looking waiters and harassed-looking waitresses rushed in and out carrying pieces of crockery and cutlery.

Overseeing everything was the Maitre'd – a tall swarthy chap, with a nose like a door wedge, hair like a black leather pancake and a moustache that looked as if he was holding a pencil between his nose and upper lip. It was his job to make sure that everything went smoothly.

Christine sat at the head of the table. Above her, held by its single golden cord, dangled the Speen Spleen. On either side of her sat the Mayor and Mayoress

resplendant in their magnificent chains of
office, encrusted with precious gems.
Christine's parents were a bit further down

the table, sitting either side of the man
from *Who's Trousers?*

They had just asked him if he'd ever held
up his own trousers on *Who's Trousers?* but
he was having difficulty understanding them
through their coveralls.

Then everyone stood, raised their glasses to Christine and sang the traditional song of the Queen of Speen (not to be confused with the traditional song of the Queen of Spain, which is almost the same except it's in Spanish). The song went as follows:

She is the Queen of Speen,
The Queeniest Speen Queen,
She's underneath the Spleen . . . OH,
Most wonderous Queen of Speen.

Christine had never felt so happy. She leant her ironing board against the table beside her, slipped her iron under her chair and thought about the year ahead – the fame, the fortune . . . the soap.

Mrs Pristine wiped away a tear . . . which wasn't the easiest of things to do whilst wearing a *Pristine Clothes Coverall*, but she managed by poking a tissue through the eyehole on the end of a fork.

A Flying Pepper Pot

As the song finished, everyone sat down.
Now, Christine hadn't noticed this, but
when she'd leant her ironing board against
the table it had inadvertently brushed
against her large silver fork, turning it
around so that the prongy bit was now
facing towards her. Not
only that, but the handle
was now wedged just
underneath the base of a
very large bone china
pepperpot.

Which all would have been
quite fine and absolutely alright
if the next unfortunate thing hadn't
happened."

"What was that Grannie?" asked Annie.
A cloud passed over the sun.

"When she sat down . . ." said Grannie,
in her most dark and mysterious of voices,
"she put . . . her elbows on the table."
Annie's eyes widened.

"Her right elbow was fine and leaned comfortably on the soft linen tablecloth. But the left one landed fairly and squarely on the prongy bit of the fork, causing the handle of the fork to jerk upwards, launching the very large bone china pepperpot up into the air.

Everyone looked up. For a few seconds the pepperpot hovered there, like a bird in flight . . . then suddenly it came down. Faster and faster it fell until it landed on the table and smashed into a thousand tiny pieces.

Pepper shot in all directions, over the walls, over the floor, and into the face of everyone sitting at that table. Everyone, that is, except Christine Pristine.

What happened next is still talked of in whispers and sung about in Speen folk songs . . ."

"What *did* happen next?" asked Annie.

"Well . . ." whispered Grannie, removing the tea cosy from the teapot. "One by one they all started to sneeze. Small polite sneezes at first, but getting bigger and more powerful, until they were all sneezing great big enormous, grown-up, scary sneezes that

blew serviettes across the table and
butterpats against the wall.

Everyone everywhere seemed to be
sneezing: the Mayor, the Mayoress, the
Maitre'd, even the man from *Who's
Trousers?* who sneezed so hard he blew
poor Lord Scrickett-Ground's wig off.

'My hair!!' cried his lordship, grabbing
the nearest thing he could and putting it on
his head. (The nearest thing to Lord
Scrickett-Ground at that
moment was a large
green lettuce leaf
which, if the truth were
known, actually looked
better than his wig.)

The wig zoomed across the room like a jet-
propelled gerbil, landing smartly on the
shoulder of a small dark-haired waitress.
Now, this wouldn't have been quite so bad
if the small dark-haired waitress hadn't just

arrived in the room holding an enormous tureen of green pea soup. She looked down at the rather furry, manky-looking thing that had just landed on her shoulder, and did what anyone else might have done under the circumstances: she screamed, threw her hands in the air and ran out of the room.

This left the giant tureen of green pea soup with nothing to hold it up but AIR . . . and air's not very good at holding things up, especially great big heavy things.

The tureen fell to the ground with the biggest crash that most people had ever heard.

Great splodges of green pea soup flew everywhere just as two more waitresses arrived, each holding huge tureens of . . . more soup!

The first waitress stepped straight into the empty tureen . .

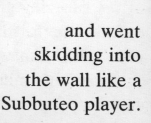

and went skidding into the wall like a Subbuteo player.

The second slipped on the soup, turned a
complete somersault and crash-landed on top
of the Maitre'd, knocking
the poor man out
senseless.

Soup was all over the place . . . down the
walls, across the floor and around the feet
of the sneezing guests, which was very
unfortunate for the four waiters who had
just arrived through the flippy-floppy doors,
each carrying a large jug of specially dyed
green cream.

One by one they stepped *slap, bang, squelch* into the room and they all looked very surprised indeed to suddenly find their legs flying up in the air in front of them like can-can dancers.

Now, you don't often see can-can dancers carrying large jugs of cream, especially green cream. It's actually listed as one of  the ten most dangerous things to do whilst can-can dancing and there's a very good reason for this:

THE CREAM FLIES EVERYWHERE,

which is exactly what happened. So now, not only were the poor guests sneezing themselves silly *and* trying to keep their very best shoes out of the slurpy soup, they were also being splattered with green cream by four completely out-of-control waiters, whose legs were now spinning round like aeroplane propellers.

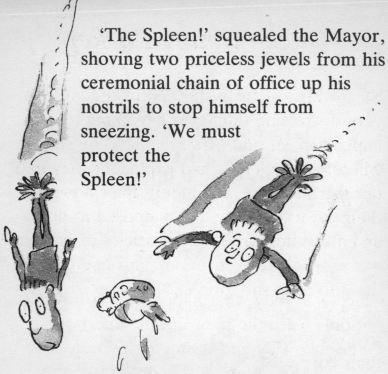

'The Spleen!' squealed the Mayor, shoving two priceless jewels from his ceremonial chain of office up his nostrils to stop himself from sneezing. 'We must protect the Spleen!'

Under the Spleen sat Christine Pristine, glancing nervously at the flying green cream and frantically polishing her choc'n'bogey mirror.

Queen Smart Porker

Meanwhile, at the other end of the table, a very distressing thing was beginning to happen to Mr and Mrs Pristine. You see, when the pepperpot had exploded, they had put the nose, eye and mouth flaps down on their coveralls (as you're supposed to do in an emergency) but a few particles of pepper had managed to get inside. This had caused them to start sneezing and, because there was nowhere for the sneezes to go, their coveralls were beginning to fill up with hot, sneezy air.

Slowly, Christine Pristine's poor parents began to float up towards the ceiling.

Down below, things were not looking good. Quite a few of the guests had slipped under the table and were slithering about in the slimy soup, desperately trying to get up again. Those that were still sitting down were either being sneezed over by the person next to them, or being splattered with cream by the high-kicking waiters . . . one of which had just gone down into a very nasty full-front splits and tipped the last of his cream over the man from *Who's Trousers?*

At the head of the table sat Christine Pristine looking even cleaner than when she'd arrived that afternoon. You know, it's a spooky thing, but not one particle of pepper, not one slop of soup and not one clot of cream had gone anywhere near her. She smiled her smug little smile and wondered if she should set up her ironing board and give the hem of her dress a quick press.

On either side of her sat the Mayor and Mayoress. The Mayoress had fallen face down in the mint sauce, and the Mayor had wedged the jewels from his ceremonial chain of office so far up his nostrils, he was having a lot of trouble pulling them out again.

Well, at least nothing else can go wrong......

..Can it?

"Hfrgbmph . . .' wailed Mr and Mrs
Pristine from way up on the ceiling. Neither
of them had the faintest idea what was
going on. But inside the hot sneezy
darkness of his coverall, Mr Pristine knew
what he must do . . .

He must feel his way towards the large
Speen chandelier, pull off one of the jaggy
crystals that hung down from it, and,
finding his good lady wife whom he knew
to be floating nearby, give *her* coverall a
quick jab, then his own, and then they
would both float back down to earth like
two freshly popped balloons.
Unfortunately, due to Mr Pristine's limited
vision through his closed eye flaps, it was

going to be pretty difficult telling the difference between a big fat floating lady angel and a big fat floating Mrs Pristine . . . but he was going to have a try.

Despite the fact that she now looked as if she was wearing a shiny green balaclava helmet (due to the large amounts of soup that had landed on her head), Queen Smart Porker was feeling very smug . . . and this was why: Christine Pristine had almost certainly ruined her own chances of being crowned Queen Clean of Speen. So, with any luck at all, Queen Smart Porker and her even smarter pigs, might very well be reinstated for yet another year. She smiled slowly, wiped a blob of soup from the end of her nose and began to recite her acceptance speech.

My porkers and I....

Now, talking of porkers . . . Unbeknown to all those people slithering around in the slurpy, sloppy, soupy mess in the Speen Golden Parlour, piggy snouts were starting to twitch outside. You see, when you mix pepper and green pea soup and green cream all together and get a lot of people to slither about in it in their very best clothes, the smell that's created is very similar to something that pigs like very much indeed . . ."

"What's that Grannie?" asked Annie.

Grannie smiled knowingly. "PIGSLOPS," she said.

"Oh," said Annie.

"Now, Queen Smart Porker's pigs had been standing around all afternoon, behaving very well and very smartly. But when that wonderful whiff began to waft towards them, their snouts started twitching . . . their mouths started watering . . . and their curly tails began to twirl round like corkscrews.

In their heart of piggy hearts those porkers knew they should really stay in their gold-sprayed piggy pigsty, but the thought of a good slurp of sloppy old pigslops was pushing all their smart thoughts away.

Meanwhile . . . high up on the Golden Parlour ceiling, Mr Pristine had managed to find his way to the chandelier, grab one of the jaggy crystal things and was now jabbing it about trying to find Mrs Pristine. Unfortunately, all this jabbing was doing terrible things to the ceiling, which was falling down in beautifully painted clumps onto the people below.

Suddenly there
was a rumbling sound.
Lord Scrickett-Ground
heard it from underneath
his lettuce leaf.

THUNDER?

ELEPHANTS?

The man from *Who's
Trousers?* heard it from
underneath his cream
jug.

EARTHQUAKE?

Mr and Mrs
Pristine heard it from
inside their coveralls.

Queen Smart Porker
heard it and
immediately knew
what it was . . .

The pigs burst into
the Golden Parlour,
snorting and slurping
away at everything in sight. Their mistress
looked on helplessly as the exhausted guests
scrambled in all directions to escape the
sniffing snouts of her porky
pride and
joy.

The Mayor began to shed a small tear. There had probably never been a room as spectacularly ruined as Speen's Golden Parlour was that day. The ceilings, the floor, the carvings, the paintings, the chandelier, not to mention the guests' finest finery. The only thing that remained unscathed by the chain of events that had been triggered off by Christine Pristine's elbow was the Speen Spleen.

The Speen Spleen

Suddenly the Mayor became aware of a loud chinking noise. It sounded as if someone was trying to get everyone's attention by hitting a glass with a spoon. The sound was coming from the direction of Christine Pristine. One by one, everyone began to quieten down and look in her direction.

When the room was in total silence, Christine Pristine put the spoon down by the side of the glass and got to her feet. She seemed to shine out from amidst the writhing mass of slime like a gleaming, green angel.

'She's going to apologise,' muttered a Lord.

'She's going to say sorry,' whispered a Lady.

'She's only a girl,' whittered a waitress. 'She wasn't to know . . .'

Christine stood at the head of the table as neat and tidy and as clean and pristine as she had been when she'd arrived. She looked slowly round the room. Everyone's eyes were on her. She took a deep breath and opened her mouth to speak . . . And do you know what she said . . . to all of those people in that room?"

Annie shook her head slowly.

"She said:

At that moment, Mr Pristine gave one last hard jab at what he thought was Mrs Pristine and sliced clean through the golden cord that held up the Spleen of Speen. The Spleen plummeted down towards the table at a frightening speed. Everyone gasped.

Now, if you've ever been sitting all alone on a see-saw when someone much bigger than you comes along and jumps on the other end . . . you'll guess what happened next. The solid gold Spleen hit the table with such force it tipped it right up. This catapulted every single thing that was on it up into the air.

The root vegetable arrangements, the sauces, the cream, the soup, the pepper, a few pigs . . . and of course, the life-size moulded greengage jelly of this year's Queen of Speen. Everyone in the room held their breath and watched in horrified astonishment as this great mass of mess hovered in the air.

And then it fell . . . down, down, down and then . . .

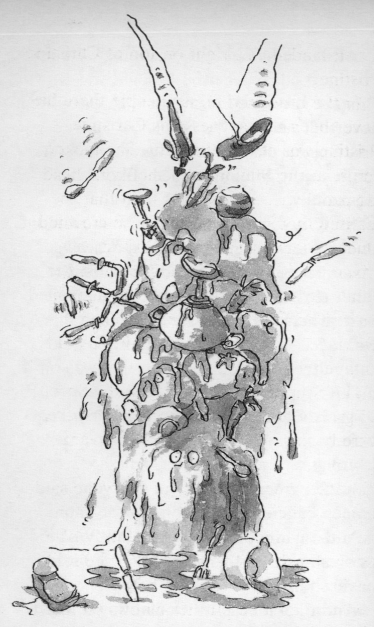

BANG! SLAP! SQUELCH!

. . . it landed . . . right on top of Christine Pristine.

In the history of messy people there has never been one as messy as Christine Pristine was at that moment. She looked across at the Mayor, who shook his head mournfully . . . and it was then that she realised that she would never be crowned Queen Clean of Speen. She'd lost her crown, she'd lost her title, she'd lost her year's supply of soap, but worse than all that, she'd ruined the Speen Golden Parlour . . . and that could never be forgiven.

The Speen Bagpipers played the Speen Disgrace Song as Christine and her parents were banished from Speen . . . never to return . . .

. . . and do you know what everyone said as she walked by?"

Annie had a pretty good idea. "We're neat and tidy and yo-or no-ot?" she said.

"Absolutely . . . and all because Christine Pristine put her elbows on the table . . ."

"So, who became the Queen of Speen then Grannie?" asked Annie.

"Ah, yes . . . the title then went to little Lucy Shooker who'd managed to keep her socks pulled up for longer than three hours."

"Wow!" sighed Annie. "What a story. But it's not *really* true is it Grannie? I mean there's not *really* a place called Speen . . . and someone called Christine Pristine and people who wear clothes called coveralls . . . is there?"

Grannie looked across at Annie and smiled ever so slightly.

"Come over here a minute," she said,

and getting creakily to her feet, she lead Annie towards an old chest of drawers.

"Open the bottom draw and pull out what you find inside . . ."

Annie bent down and pulled the drawer open. Inside she saw something sort of shiny and plastic with flowers on. She began to pull it out.

"What is it, Grannie?"

"Well, you remember I said Christine Pristine's mother sold *two Pristine Clothes Coveralls*."

"Oh yes, one was to her dad . . . and one . . ." Annie looked down at what she was holding. It had two eyeholes, a nosehole and a mouthhole and it was completely person-shaped. Annie looked round at Grannie.

"Of course . . ." began Grannie, "I would have preferred it to have had a nice root vegetable pattern . . ."

She prodded the flowery coverall with her finger.

"I'll never put my elbows on the table again," said Annie . . .

And she never did.

Also in Puffin

TALES FROM THE SHOP THAT NEVER SHUTS
Martin Waddell

McGlone lives at the Shop that Never Shuts, and Flash and Buster Cook are in McGlone's Gang with wee Biddy O'Hare. In these five highly entertaining stories the Gang dig for Viking treasure, are frightened that a sea monster has eaten Biddy, discover that McGlone needs glasses, look after the Shop that Never Shuts on their own, and give Biddy a birthday party.

VERA PRATT AND THE BALD HEAD
Brough Girling

When Wally Pratt and his fanatic mechanic mother enter the Motorbike and Sidecar Grand Prix, nothing is really as it seems. Vera's old enemy, Captain Smoothy-Smythe, is up to his old tricks and suddenly Wally is kidnapped. Rescue him? She can't do that yet, she's got to win the Grand Prix first. Two minutes to go and Vera finds herself the ideal partner – a headmaster with no hair!

CRUMMY MUMMY AND ME
Anne Fine

How would you feel if your mother had royal-blue hair and wore lavender fishnet tights? It's not easy for Minna being the only sensible one in the family, even though she's used to her mum's weird clothes and eccentric behaviour. But then the whole family are a bit unusual, and their exploits make very entertaining and enjoyable reading.

SON OF A GUN
Janet and Allan Ahlberg

A galloping, riotous wild west farce in which the plot thickens with every page until a combined force of Indians, US cavalry, old-timers, dancing-girls and the eight-year-old hero are racing to the rescue of a mother and baby, besieged in their cabin by two incompetent bandits called Slocum. As one of the Slocums says, 'Cavalry *and* Indians? Where's the fairness in that?' – *The New Statesman*

HENRY AND RIBSY
Beverly Cleary

Henry's dream is to go fishing with his father. He can just see himself sitting in a boat, reeling in an enormous salmon. Mr Huggins has promised he will take Henry fishing on one condition: that he keeps Ribsy out of trouble and does not let him annoy the neighbours, especially Mr Grumble next door. The trouble is, keeping a dog like Ribsy under control isn't that easy!

WILL THE REAL GERTRUDE HOLLINGS PLEASE STAND UP?
Sheila Greenwald

Gertrude is in a bad way. She's a bit slow at school but everyone thinks she's dumb and her teachers call her 'Learning Disabled' behind her back. As if this isn't enough, her parents go off on a business trip leaving her with her aunt and uncle and her obnoxious cousin, Albert – a 'superachiever'. Gertrude is determined to win Perfect Prize-Winning Albert's respect by whatever means it takes . . .